HUMPHREY C

Mr Maj

Illustrated by Frank Rodgers

PUFFIN

Contents

*With thanks to Class 7 at Marlborough Primary School,
Chelsea, for their help, and especially Lucy Tsancheva,
who thought of most of Chapters 7 and 8.*

PUFFIN BOOKS

Published by the Penguin Group
Penguin Books Ltd, 80 Strand, London WC2R 0RL, England
Penguin Group (USA) Inc., 375 Hudson Street, New York, New York 10014, USA
Penguin Group (Canada), 90 Eglinton Avenue East, Suite 700, Toronto, Ontario, Canada M4P 2Y3
(a division of Pearson Penguin Canada Inc.)
Penguin Ireland, 25 St Stephen's Green, Dublin 2, Ireland (a division of Penguin Books Ltd)
Penguin Group (Australia), 250 Camberwell Road, Camberwell,
Victoria 3124, Australia (a division of Pearson Australia Group Pty Ltd)
Penguin Books India Pvt Ltd, 11 Community Centre,
Panchsheel Park, New Delhi – 110 017, India
Penguin Group (NZ), cnr Airborne and Rosedale Roads, Albany,
Auckland 1310, New Zealand (a division of Pearson New Zealand Ltd)
Penguin Books (South Africa) (Pty) Ltd, 24 Sturdee Avenue,
Rosebank, Johannesburg 2196, South Africa

Penguin Books Ltd, Registered Offices: 80 Strand, London WC2R 0RL, England

www.penguin.com

First published by Kestrel Books 1984
Published in Puffin Books 1985
002

This edition published 2006 for Index Books Ltd

Filmset in Palatino

Made and printed in England by Clays Ltd, St Ives plc

British Library Cataloguing in Publication Data
A CIP catalogue record for this book is available from the British Library

ISBN-13: 978–0–141–34698–4

www.greenpenguin.co.uk

MIX
Paper from
responsible sources
FSC
www.fsc.org   FSC™ C018179

Penguin Books is committed to a sustainable
future for our business, our readers and our planet.
This book is made from Forest Stewardship
Council™ certified paper.

1. The Carpet-Bicycle

It was Monday morning, it was pouring with rain, and it was everyone's first day back at St Barty's Primary School after the Christmas holidays. That's why Class Three were in a bad temper.

Pandora Green had been rude to Melanie, so Melanie was crying (though Melanie always found *something* to cry about). Hamish Bigmore was trying to pick a quarrel with Thomas and Pete, the twins. And Mr Potter the head teacher was very cross because the new teacher for Class Three hadn't turned up.

'I can't think where he is,' he grumbled at Class Three. 'He should have been here at nine o'clock for the beginning of school. And now it's nearly ten, and I should be teaching Class Two. We'll have to open the folding doors and let you share the lesson with them.'

Class Three groaned. They thought themselves very important people, and didn't in the least want to share a lesson with Class Two, who were just babies.

'Bother this thing,' muttered Mr Potter, struggling with the folding doors that separated the classrooms.

'*I'll* help you, Mr Potter,' said Hamish Bigmore, who didn't really want to help at all, but just to be a nuisance as usual. And then everyone else began to shout: 'Don't let

Hamish Bigmore do it, he's no good, let *me* help,' so that in a moment there was uproar.

But suddenly silence fell. And there was a gasp.

Mr Potter was still fiddling with the folding doors, so he didn't see what was happening. But Class Three did.

One of the big windows in the classroom slid open all by itself, and *something* flew in.

It was a man on a magic carpet.

There could be no doubt about that. Class Three knew a magic carpet when they saw one. After all, they'd read *Aladdin* and all that sort of stuff. There are magic carpets all over the place in *Aladdin*. But this wasn't *Aladdin*. This was St Barty's Primary School on a wet Monday morning. And magic carpets don't turn up in schools. Class Three knew that. So they stared.

The carpet hung in the air for a moment, as if it wasn't sure what to do. Then it came down on the floor with a bump. 'Ow!' said the man sitting on it.

He was quite old, and he had a pointed beard and very bright eyes, behind a pair of glasses. His hair and clothes were wet from the rain. On the whole he looked quite ordinary — except for the fact that he was sitting on a magic carpet.

'I just can't manage it,' said Mr Potter, still pushing at the folding doors. 'I'll have to go and get the caretaker.'

Then he saw the man on the carpet.

'What – how – eh?' said Mr Potter. Words usually deserted Mr Potter at difficult moments.

The man on the carpet scrambled to his feet. 'Majeika,' he said politely, offering his hand.

Mr Potter took the hand. 'Majeika?' he repeated, puzzled. Then a look of understanding dawned on his face. 'Ah,' he said, 'Mr Majeika!' He turned to Class Three. 'Boys and girls,' he said, 'I want you to meet Mr Majeika. He's your new teacher.'

For a moment there was silence. Then Melanie began to cry: 'Boo-hoo! I'm *frightened* of him! He came on a magic carpet!'

'What's the matter, Melanie?' snapped Mr Potter. 'I can't hear a word you're saying. It sounded like "magic carpet" or some such nonsense.' He turned briskly to Mr Majeika. 'Now, you're rather late, Mr Majeika. You might have telephoned me.'

'I'm so sorry,' said Mr Majeika. 'You see, my magic carpet took a wrong turning. It's normally quite good at finding the way, but I think the rain must have got into it. I do beg your pardon.'

'Never mind,' said Mr Potter. 'And now ... Wait a minute, did I hear you say *magic carpet*?'

It was Mr Majeika's turn to look bothered. 'Oh, did I really say that? How very silly of me. A complete slip of the tongue. I meant — *bicycle*, of course. I came on a bicycle.'

'Quite so,' said Mr Potter. 'Bicycle, of course...' His voice tailed off. He was staring at the magic carpet. 'What's that?' he said rather faintly.

'That?' said Mr Majeika cheerily. 'That's

my magic — ' He cleared his throat. 'Oh dear,
my mistake again. *That's my bicycle.*' And as
he said these last words, he pointed a finger
at the magic carpet.

There was a funny sort of humming noise,
and the carpet rolled itself up and turned into
a bicycle.

Mr Majeika leant cheerily against the
handlebars and rang the bicycle bell. 'Nice
bike, isn't it?' he said, smiling at Mr Potter.

You could have heard a pin drop.

Mr Potter turned rather white. 'I – I don't think I feel very well,' he said at last. 'I – I don't seem to be able to tell the difference between a carpet and a bicycle.'

Mr Majeika smiled even more cheerily. 'Never mind, a very easy mistake to make. And now I think it's time I began to teach our young friends here.'

Mr Potter wiped his forehead with his handkerchief. 'What? Oh – yes – of course,' he muttered faintly, backing to the door. 'Yes, yes, please do begin. Can't tell a bicycle from a carpet . . .' he mumbled to himself as he left the room.

'Now then,' said Mr Majeika to Class Three, 'to work!'

2. Chips for Everyone

Never had Class Three been so quiet as they were for the rest of that lesson. They sat in absolute silence as Mr Majeika told them what work he planned to give them for the rest of that term.

Not that any of them was really listening to what he was saying. It actually sounded very ordinary, with stuff about nature-study, and the kings and queens of England, and special projects, and that sort of thing, just like all the other teachers. But they couldn't take it in. Each of them was thinking about just one thing: the magic carpet.

When break came, and they were all having milk and biscuits, they whispered about it.

'I *saw* it,' whispered Pandora Green's best friend Jody.

'So did I,' said Thomas and Pete together. 'It *was* a magic carpet.'

'If you ask *me*,' said Hamish Bigmore, 'it was a mass hallucination.' Hamish Bigmore was always learning long words just so that he could show them off.

'What's that mean?' said Thomas and Pete suspiciously.

'It's when you think you've seen something and you haven't,' said Hamish Bigmore. 'People get them when they're walking across the desert. They think they see a pool of water, and when they get there, there's only sand.'

'But we're not in the desert, you idiot,' said Thomas. 'And we didn't see water, we saw a magic carpet, and it turned into a bicycle. And we *all* saw it, so how could we have imagined it?'

'That's why it's called *mass* hallucination,' said Hamish Bigmore grandly. '*Mass* means lots of people. So idiot yourself!'

And they might have believed him, if it wasn't for what happened at dinner.

Most of Class Three ate school dinner, but some of them were sent to school with packed lunches which their mothers had made at home, and which they ate at a separate table. Thomas and Pete did this, and so did Jody.

So did Wim. He was Thomas and Pete's younger brother. He was in the nursery class, so Thomas and Pete only saw him at dinner time. He was really called William, but 'Wim' was how he said his own name, so that was what everyone called him.

Wim was tucking happily into a piece of egg and bacon flan, which was his favourite lunch. Thomas and Pete were talking to Jody while they ate theirs. 'What do you think about the magic carpet?' they asked her for the hundredth time.

'Ssh, here he comes!' whispered Jody.

Mr Majeika was approaching their table. He sat down next to them. 'Hello,' he said in a friendly manner. 'Was there anything you wanted to ask me about the lessons for this term?'

Thomas, Pete and Jody looked at each other. Of course there was something they wanted to ask him!

Suddenly there was a wail from Wim. He had dropped his egg and bacon flan on the floor.

Thomas and Pete looked gloomily at each other. They would have to give Wim some of their own dinner.

'My poor chap, most unfortunate,' said Mr Majeika. He bent down and picked up the mess of egg and bacon flan. 'We must see what we can do with this,' he said to Wim. 'Tell me, my young friend, what is your favourite food?'

Wim thought for a moment. Then he said: 'Chips.'

'Ah,' said Mr Majeika, shutting his eyes

for a moment, and pointing at Wim's plate.
'Chips.'

'Oo!' said Wim suddenly. And no wonder,
for on his plate, where the broken bits of flan
had been, stood a huge pile of steaming hot
chips.

'Oh!' said Thomas, Pete and Jody.

'Would you like some too, my young
friends?' said Mr Majeika. Thomas, Pete and
Jody nodded, and suddenly, out of nowhere,
there were piles of chips on their plates too.

'Gosh!' said Thomas, Pete and Jody.

Suddenly another voice broke in. 'What's
this? You know we don't allow chips here at
dinner time.' It was Mr Potter.

He had come up behind Mr Majeika
without anyone noticing. 'It's a very strict
rule,' he said. 'Parents may send their
children to school with sandwiches or other
cold food, but I will not allow boys and girls

to go out and buy chips during the dinner
hour.'

'But we didn't buy them,' began Thomas.

'No, no,' interrupted Mr Majeika quickly.
'They certainly didn't buy them. It was *I* who
provided them, not knowing the school
rules. It won't happen again.'

'Well,' said Mr Potter crossly, 'please don't
let it.' He walked off.

Mr Majeika sighed. 'Oh dear,' he said, 'I
think I've got a lot to learn in my new job.

You see, I'm not at all experienced at being a teacher. I've always worked as, well ... something else.'

Thomas hesitated for a moment, then plucked up courage to say: 'Do you mean you were a *wizard*?'

Mr Majeika nodded. 'I might as well admit it,' he said. 'I worked as one for years, but then I began to get a bit rusty on my spells, and recently there hasn't been much business. People don't believe much in wizards nowadays, so naturally they don't often pay them to do some work. So in the end I just had to get another kind of job. That's why I'm here. And now I really *must* remember that I'm a teacher, and not a wizard at all. And you must all help me. You mustn't try to persuade me to do any – ' He hesitated.

'Any magic?' said Pete.

Mr Majeika nodded. 'You must let me be an *ordinary teacher*,' he said. 'Do you promise?'

They all nodded. But each of them thought it would be a very difficult promise to keep.

*

By three-fifteen that day, when afternoon school was nearly at an end, nothing else out of the ordinary had happened in Class Three. In fact the afternoon would have ended very boringly if it hadn't been for Hamish Bigmore.

Hamish had been put to sit next to Melanie, which was a bad thing for Melanie, as Hamish liked nothing better than to make her cry.

Sure enough, when there were only a few more minutes to go, Melanie started to sob. 'Boo-hoo! Hamish Bigmore is jabbing me with his ruler!'

Hamish Bigmore said he wasn't, but Mr Majeika moved fast enough to get to the scene of the crime before Hamish had time to hide the ruler. 'Put it down!' said Mr Majeika.

'Shan't,' said Hamish Bigmore.

There was silence, and everyone in Class Three remembered how Hamish Bigmore had refused to do as he was told by last term's teacher. It was mostly because of him that she had left the school.

'Put it down,' said Mr Majeika again.

'Shan't,' said Hamish Bigmore for a second time.

'Then,' said Mr Majeika slowly, *I shall make you wish very much that you had put it down.*'

And Hamish Bigmore screamed.

'A snake! Help! Help!' he shouted. And there fell from his hand something that certainly wasn't a ruler.

It was a long grey-green snake with patterned markings and a forked tongue. Its mouth was open and it was hissing.

In a moment everyone else was shouting too, and clambering on to the desks, and doing anything they could to get out of its reach. But not Mr Majeika.

He stepped calmly up to the snake, knelt down, and picked it up. And as his hand touched it, it turned back into a ruler.

'What are you frightened of?' he asked Hamish Bigmore. 'This is only your ruler. But perhaps next time you will do as you are told.'

He gave the ruler back to Hamish Bigmore, who dropped it fearfully on his desk and shrank away from it.

A moment later the bell rang, and school was over for the day. Class Three usually rushed outside as soon as they heard the bell. But today they were quiet as mice.

'He *said* he didn't want to do any magic,' said Thomas to Pete on the way home.

'I think he just forgets about that now and then,' said Pete. 'After all, if you've been a wizard for years, it can't be easy stopping overnight.'

'Mr Majeika...' said Thomas thoughtfully to himself. 'Do you know, I don't think that's his real name.'

'No,' said Pete. 'I think he ought to be called Mr Magic.'

3. *Hamish Goes Swimming*

In fact for a long time after that Mr Magic, as all Class Three were soon calling him, *didn't* forget that he was meant to be a teacher, and not a wizard. Nothing peculiar happened for weeks and weeks, and the lessons went on just as they would have with any other teacher. The magic carpet, the chips, and the snake seemed like a dream.

Then Hamish Bigmore came to stay at Thomas and Pete's house.

This wasn't at all a good thing, at least not for Thomas and Pete. But they had no choice. Hamish Bigmore's mother and father had to go away for a few days, and Thomas and Pete's mum had offered to look after Hamish until they came back. She never asked Thomas and Pete what they thought about the idea until it was too late.

Hamish Bigmore behaved even worse than they had expected. He found all their favourite books and games, which they had tried to hide from him, and spoilt them or left them lying about the house where they got trodden on and broken. He pulled the stuffing out of Wim's favourite teddy bear, bounced up and down so hard on the garden climbing-frame that it bent, and talked for hours and hours after the light had been put out at night, so that Thomas and Pete couldn't get to sleep. 'It's awful,' said Thomas. 'I wish that something really nasty would happen to him.'

And it did.

Hamish Bigmore was behaving just as badly at school as at Thomas and Pete's house. The business of the ruler turning into a snake had frightened him for a few days, but no longer than that, and now he was up to his old tricks again, doing anything rather than listen to Mr Majeika and behave properly.

On the Wednesday morning before Hamish Bigmore's mother and father were due to come home, Mr Majeika was giving Class Three a nature-study lesson, with the tadpoles in the glass tank that sat by his desk. Hamish Bigmore was being ruder than ever.

'Does anyone know how long tadpoles take to turn into frogs?' Mr Majeika asked Class Three.

'Haven't the slightest idea,' said Hamish Bigmore.

'Please,' said Melanie, holding up her hand, 'I don't think it's very long. Only a few weeks.'

'*You* should know,' sneered Hamish Bigmore. 'You look just like a tadpole yourself.'

Melanie began to cry.

'Be quiet, Hamish Bigmore,' said Mr Majeika. 'Melanie is quite right. It all happens very quickly. The tadpoles grow arms and legs, and very soon —'

'I shouldn't think they'll grow at all if they see *you* staring in at them through the glass,' said Hamish Bigmore to Mr Majeika. 'Your face would frighten them to death!'

'Hamish Bigmore, I have had enough of you,' said Mr Majeika. 'Will you stop behaving like this?'

'No, I won't!' said Hamish Bigmore.

Mr Majeika pointed a finger at him.

And Hamish Bigmore vanished.

There was complete silence. Class Three stared at the empty space where Hamish Bigmore had been sitting.

Then Pandora Green pointed at the glass tank, and began to shout: 'Look! Look! A frog! A frog! One of the tadpoles has turned into a frog!'

Mr Majeika looked closely at the tank. Then he put his head in his hands. He seemed very upset.

'No, Pandora,' he said. 'It isn't one of the tadpoles. It's Hamish Bigmore.'

For a moment, Class Three were struck dumb. Then everyone burst out laughing. 'Hooray! Hooray! Hamish Bigmore has been turned into a frog! Good old Mr Magic!'

'It looks like Hamish Bigmore, doesn't it?' Pete said to Thomas. Certainly the frog's expression looked very much like Hamish's face. And it was splashing noisily around the tank and carrying on in the silly sort of way that Hamish did.

Mr Majeika looked very worried. 'Oh dear, oh dear,' he kept saying.

'Didn't you mean to do it?' asked Jody.

Mr Majeika shook his head. 'Certainly not. I quite forgot myself. It was a complete mistake.'

'Well,' said Thomas, 'you can turn him back again, can't you?'

Mr Majeika shook his head again. 'I'm not at all sure that I can,' he said.

Thomas and Pete looked at him in astonishment.

'You see,' he went on, 'it was an old spell, something I learnt years and years ago and thought I'd forgotten. I don't know what were the exact words I used. And, as I am sure you understand, it's not possible to undo a spell unless you know exactly what the words were.'

'So Hamish Bigmore may have to stay a

frog?' said Pete. 'That's the best thing I've heard for ages!'

Mr Majeika shook his head. 'For you, maybe, but not for him. I'll have to try and do *something*.' And he began to mutter a whole series of strange-sounding words under his breath.

All kinds of things began to happen. The room went dark, and the floor seemed to rock. Green smoke came out of an empty jar on Mr Majeika's desk. He tried some more words, and this time there was a small thunderstorm in the sky outside. But nothing happened to the frog.

'Oh, dear,' sighed Mr Majeika, 'what *am* I going to do?'

4. The Frog's Princess

Thomas and Pete thought for a moment. Then Thomas said: 'Don't worry about it yet, Mr Magic. Hamish Bigmore's parents are away, and he's staying with us. You've got two days to find the right spell before they come back and expect to find him.'

'Two days,' repeated Mr Majeika. 'In that case there is a chance. We shall simply have to see what happens at midnight.'

'Midnight?' asked Jody.

'My friend,' said Mr Majeika, 'surely you know that in fairy stories everything returns to its proper shape when the clock strikes twelve?'

'Cinderella's coach,' said Jody.

'Exactly,' answered Mr Majeika. 'But one can't be certain of it. There's only a chance. I'll stay here tonight, and see what happens.'

And with that, Class Three went home.

Thomas and Pete felt that really they should have taken Hamish Bigmore home with them, even if he *was* a frog. After all, he was supposed to be staying with them.

34

'But,' said Pete, 'it's not easy carrying frogs. He might escape, and jump into a river or something, and we'd never see him again.'

'And a very good thing too,' said Thomas.

'You can't say that,' remarked Pete. 'He may be only Hamish Bigmore to you and me, but to his mum and dad he's darling little Hamie, or something like that. And just think what it would be like to be mother and father to a frog. Going to the shops, and the library, and that sort of thing, and people saying: "Oh, Mrs Bigmore, what a *sweet* little frog you're carrying in that jar." And Hamish's mum having to say: "Oh, Mrs Smith, that's not just a frog, that's our son Hamish."'

When Thomas and Pete's mum saw them at the school gates the first thing she said was 'Where's Hamish?', and they had quite a time persuading her that Hamish wouldn't be coming home with them that afternoon, or staying the night, but was visiting friends, and was being perfectly well taken care of.

'Who are these friends?' she asked suspiciously. 'What's their name?'

'Tadpoles,' said Pete, without thinking.

'Idiot,' whispered Thomas, kicking him. 'We don't know their name,' he told his mum. 'But Mr Majeika, our new teacher, arranged it, so it must be all right.'

'Oh, did he?' said their mum. 'Well, he might have told me. But I suppose I shouldn't fuss.' And she took them home.

When they got back to school the next morning, Hamish Bigmore was still a frog.

'Nothing happened at all,' said Mr Majeika gloomily.

He tried to make Class Three get on with their ordinary work, but it wasn't much use. Nobody had their minds on anything but Hamish Bigmore, swimming up and down in his tank.

Everyone kept making suggestions to Mr Majeika.

'Mr Magic, couldn't you just get a magic wand and wave it over him?'

'Couldn't you say "Abracadabra" and see if that works?'

'Couldn't you find another wizard and ask him what to do?'

'My friends,' said Mr Majeika, 'it's no use. There's nothing else to try. Last night, while I was here alone, I made use of every possible means I know, and I can do nothing. And as to finding another wizard, that would be very hard indeed. There are so very few still working, and we don't know each other's names. It might take me years to find another one, and even then he might not have the answer.'

Class Three went home rather gloomily that day. They had all begun to feel sorry for Hamish Bigmore. 'He's staying with his friends again,' Thomas and Pete told their mother.

The next day was Friday. Hamish Bigmore's parents were due to come home that evening.

Half-way through morning school, Jody suddenly put up her hand and said: 'Mr Magic?'

'Yes, Jody?'

'Mr Magic, I've got an idea. You said that things *sometimes* happen like they do in fairy stories. I mean, like Cinderella's coach turning back into a pumpkin.'

'Yes, sometimes,' said Mr Majeika, 'but as you've seen with Hamish, not always.'

'Well,' said Jody, 'there is something that I wondered about. You see, in fairy stories people are often turned into frogs. And they always get turned back again in the end, don't they? And I've been trying to remember *how*.'

Jody paused. 'Go on,' said Mr Majeika.

'Well,' said Jody, 'I *did* remember. Frogs turn back into princes when they get kissed by a princess.'

Mr Majeika's eyes lit up. 'Goodness!' he said. 'You're absolutely right! Why didn't I think of that? We must try it at once!'

'Try what, Mr Magic?' asked Pandora Green.

'Why, have Hamish Bigmore kissed by a princess. And then I do believe there's a very good chance he will change back.'

'But please, Mr Magic,' said Thomas, 'how are you going to manage it? I mean, there's not so very many princesses around these days. Not as many as in fairy stories.'

'There's some at Buckingham Palace,' said Pandora.

'But they don't go around kissing frogs,' said Thomas.

'You bet they don't,' said Pete. 'You see pictures of them in the newspapers doing all sorts of things, opening new hospitals, and naming ships, and that sort of thing. But not kissing frogs.'

'Are you sure, my young friend?' said Mr Majeika gloomily.

'Quite sure,' said Thomas. 'Unless they do it when nobody's looking. I mean, it's not the sort of thing they'd get much fun out of, is it? Frog-kissing, I mean.'

'I bet,' said Pete, 'that a real live princess wouldn't do it if you paid her a thousand pounds.'

'Just imagine,' said Thomas, 'going to Buckingham Palace, and ringing the doorbell, and saying: "Please, have you got any princesses in today, and would they mind kissing a frog for us?" They'd probably fetch the police.'

'Oh dear,' said Mr Majeika. 'I'm afraid you're right.'

Nobody spoke for a long time. Then Mr Majeika said gloomily: 'It seems that Hamish Bigmore will have to remain a frog. I wonder what his parents will say.'

'Please,' said Jody, 'I've got an idea again. It may be silly, but it *might* work. What I think is this. If we can't get a real princess, we might *pretend* to have one. Make a kind of play, I mean. Dress up somebody like a princess. Do you think that's silly?' She looked hopefully at Mr Majeika.

'Not at all,' said Mr Majeika. 'We've nothing to lose by trying it!'

Which was how Class Three came to spend a good deal of the morning trying to make the room look like a royal palace in a fairy story. They found the school caretaker and persuaded him to lend them some old blue curtains that were used for the play at the end of term. And Mrs Honey who taught the nursery class agreed to give them a box of dressing-up clothes that the little children used. In this were several crowns and robes and other things that could be made to look royal.

Then there was a dreadful argument about who was to play the princess.

Jody said she ought to, because it had all been her idea. Pandora Green said *she* should, because she looked pretty, and princesses always look pretty. Mr Majeika tried to settle it by saying that Melanie should do it, as she was the only girl in the class who hadn't asked to. But Melanie, who hated the idea of kissing a frog, started to cry. So in the end Mr Majeika said that Jody should do it after all, and the other girls could be sort-of-princesses too, only Jody would play the chief one.

Then they got ready. A kind of throne had been made out of Mr Majeika's chair, with one of the blue curtains draped over it.

Jody wore another of the curtains as a cloak, and one of the crowns, and a lot of coloured beads from the dressing-up box. And all the other girls stood round her.

Mr Majeika turned out the classroom lights and drew the curtains. Then he said he thought they ought to have some music, just to make things seem more like a fairy story. So Thomas got out his recorder, and played 'God Save the Queen' and 'Good King Wenceslas', which were the only tunes he knew. They didn't seem quite right for the occasion, but Mr Majeika said they would have to do. Then he told Jody to start being the princess, and say the sort of things that princesses might say in fairy stories.

Jody thought for a moment. Then she said in a high voice: 'O my courtiers, I have heard that in this kingdom there is a poor prince who has been enchanted into a frog by some wicked magician.' She turned to Mr Majeika and whispered: 'You're not wicked, really, Mr Magic, but that's what happens in fairy stories, isn't it?'

'Of course,' said Mr Majeika. 'Please continue. You are doing splendidly.'

'O my courtiers,' went on Jody, 'I do request that one of you shall speedily bring me this frog. For I have seen it written that should a princess of the blood royal kiss this poor frog with her own lips, he will regain his proper shape.' She paused. 'Well, go on, somebody,' she hissed. 'Fetch me the frog!'

It was Mr Majeika himself who stepped up to the tank, put in his hands, and drew out Hamish Bigmore. So he did not see the door opening and Mr Potter coming into the room.

'Ah, Mr Majeika,' said Mr Potter, 'I just wanted to ask you if you could look after school dinner again today, because –' He stopped, staring at the extraordinary scene.

Mr Majeika was kneeling on one knee in front of Jody, holding out the frog. 'Go on,' he whispered, 'I feel the magic working.'

'O frog,' said Jody in her high voice, 'O frog, I command you, turn back into a prince!' And she kissed the frog.

'Now, really,' said Mr Potter, 'I'm not at all in favour of nature-study being mixed up with story-times. And school curtains should not be used for this sort of thing. While as to that frog, its proper place is a pond. I'll allow tadpoles in school, but not frogs. They jump out of the tanks and get all over the place. Now, if you'll just hand that one over ... Where is it?'

'Here I am,' said Hamish Bigmore. He had appeared out of nowhere, and the frog was gone.

Mr Potter sat down very suddenly in the nearest chair. 'I don't feel very well,' he said.

'Ah,' said Hamish Bigmore, 'you should try being a frog for a few days. Does you no end of good. Makes you feel really healthy, I can tell you. All that swimming about, why, I've never felt better in my life. And being kissed by princesses, too. Not that my princess was a real one.' He turned to Mr Majeika. 'You really should have taken me to Buckingham Palace,' he said. 'I'm sure the Queen herself would have done it, to oblige me.'

Mr Potter got to his feet and left the room, muttering something about needing to go and see a doctor because he was imagining things.

'And now,' said Hamish Bigmore to Class Three, 'I'm going to tell you all about the life and habits of the frog.' Which he did, at great length.

'Oh dear,' said Pete to Thomas. 'He's worse than ever.'

5. The Disappearing Bottle

It was about three weeks after this that
several of Class Three went to see a film
about Superman.

'The best bit,' said Jody to Pete and
Thomas, 'was when he flew right over those
tall buildings. I'd love to be able to fly like
that. Do you think people ever can?'

'I shouldn't have thought so,' said Pete.
'But you could ask Mr Magic. I'm sure he'd
know.'

So, when Class Three were beginning
their next lesson, Jody did ask him: 'Mr
Magic, can you really fly, like Superman?'

Mr Majeika smiled at her over his glasses.

'If you mean *me*, then certainly not! I'm too old for such things. But someone a bit younger could manage it, with a little help.'

'Do you mean a little magic?' asked Jody. Mr Majeika nodded.

'Rubbish!' shouted Hamish Bigmore. 'You couldn't make *anyone* fly, Mr Magic. No one could. It's scientifically impossible.' Since the business of the frog, Hamish Bigmore had been behaving worse than ever. Obviously he thought Mr Majeika wouldn't dare to do anything else to him.

Mr Majeika sighed wearily. 'It is not rubbish, Hamish Bigmore, but I don't intend to waste time showing you.'

'Oh do, please *do*,' said Jody, and soon there was a chorus of: 'Yes, *do*, Mr Magic! Couldn't you, just *once*?'

'Of course he can't,' sneered Hamish Bigmore.

'Very well then,' snapped Mr Majeika, 'just to prove Hamish Bigmore wrong, I will. But it will have to wait until tomorrow, when I can bring the potion.'

Everyone fell silent, wondering what 'the potion' was.

When the next day came, Mr Majeika seemed at first to have forgotten all about his promise, for he said nothing about it. At last Jody asked him: 'Did you bring the flying potion, Mr Magic?'

Mr Majeika frowned. 'Well, yes, I did. But really I think the whole idea is a mistake. I'd much rather we forgot all about it. These things have a way of getting out of hand ...'

'There you are!' jeered Hamish Bigmore. 'I told you he couldn't do it.'

'Oh, really, Hamish Bigmore, you're enough to try the patience of a witch's broomstick,' grumbled Mr Majeika. 'I suppose I'll *have* to do it just to keep you quiet.'

'Do what, Mr Magic?' asked Thomas.

'Why, give you all some of the flying potion,' said Mr Majeika.

There was a happy uproar. 'What, all of us?' asked Pete. 'Are we all going to be able to fly?'

'Well, it'll have to be all or none,' answered Mr Majeika. 'Can you imagine how jealous everyone would be if I only let one or two of you do it? But it won't be proper flying, mind. Just a little hover in the air. The potion is far too precious to be wasted.'

Class Three tried to make him change his mind and allow them to fly properly, but he wouldn't. So in the end they queued up, and were each given a very small spoonful by Mr Majeika. It was green and sticky, and tasted like a rather nice cough mixture. Only

Hamish Bigmore refused to have any; he said the whole idea was silly.

As soon as they had taken it, Class Three began to jump up and down, in the hope of taking off into the air. But nothing happened.

They were all dreadfully disappointed. 'There you are!' sneered Hamish Bigmore. 'I told you so! It doesn't work!'

'Oh, but it does,' said Mr Majeika. 'I forgot to tell you that it takes exactly half an hour before anything happens. So we must get on with the lesson for the next half hour, and *then* see.'

It was a very long, slow half hour, and even when it ended nothing happened to Class Three. 'What's gone wrong?' Jody asked Mr Majeika.

'Nothing,' answered Mr Majeika, smiling. 'You can't just sit there and expect to fly without *doing* anything.'

'Do you mean we should wave our arms about or something?' asked Pete.

Mr Majeika shook his head. 'No, my friend. The secret is to *think* about flying. If the notion of flying comes into your head, then — hey presto!'

'I'm thinking hard about it,' said Jody. 'I'm thinking about floating up in the air from my desk, and — Oh! *Oh!*' Suddenly she found herself doing just that.

In a moment they were all doing it. It was a very peculiar feeling; you simply had to think about leaving the ground, and you did. What's more, once you were in the air, if you thought about (say) spinning round like a top, you found yourself doing it. Pete said:

'I'm going to think about floating across the room to the door –' and there he was, doing just that.

The only thing that disappointed them was that they were never very far from the floor. 'Can't you let us go higher?' they pleaded with Mr Majeika.

He shook his head. 'Too risky,' he said. 'You might bump your heads on the ceiling, or do all kinds of dreadful things. And anyway, I want to save my precious flying potion. It always wears off in half an hour, however much you take, so it would be an awful waste to give you lots of it.'

Alas, it did wear off in half an hour, to everyone's regret, and all too soon they were down on the ground again, quite unable to float, however much they thought about it.

'Well, my friends,' said Mr Majeika, 'I hope you enjoyed that. And,' he turned to Hamish Bigmore, who had been sitting watching everyone else float through the air, 'I hope *you* believe me now.'

'Oh yes, Mr Magic,' answered Hamish Bigmore, with a rather peculiar smile on his face.

'Very good,' said Mr Majeika. 'Well then, let me put the potion away, and we can get on again with our proper lessons, which today —' He stopped suddenly. 'What's happened to the potion?' he said.

The bottle had vanished.

'*Where is the potion?*' said Mr Majeika again, in an anxious voice. 'It was on my desk. Someone has picked it up and hidden it. Will they please return it at once?'

No one said anything. Mr Majeika turned
to Hamish Bigmore. 'Hamish,' he said,
'somehow I have a feeling that *you* are
behind this.'

Hamish Bigmore shook his head. 'Oh, no,
Mr Majeika,' he said sweetly, 'why should *I*
do a thing like that?'

Mr Majeika looked at him steadily. 'Turn
out your pockets,' he said to Hamish. But the
bottle wasn't in Hamish's pockets.

After that, Mr Majeika searched everyone
in Class Three, saying as he did so: 'Oh dear,
I *knew* I shouldn't have brought the potion to
school. One of you has played a wretched
trick on me, and it's quite unfair.'

'Perhaps,' suggested Hamish Bigmore, 'the
bottle itself can fly, and it's flown away?' He
laughed uproariously, but Mr Majeika was
not amused.

Nowhere could the bottle be found, and

by the end of school for that day Mr Majeika was looking very worried and very cross.

'I'm sure it *is* Hamish,' said Pete to Thomas. 'He had something tucked under his coat when he left the classroom.'

'Well,' said Thomas, 'I'm sure we'll find out who's got it. Whoever they are, they're bound to start flying pretty soon.'

6. *Mr Potter Goes for a Spin*

But no one did. Days went by, then several
weeks, and nothing peculiar happened in
Class Three. After a time Mr Majeika, who at
first had continued to look very worried and
cross, stopped seeming to be so unhappy
about the loss of his potion. Eventually he
seemed to have forgotten all about it.

The weather gradually began to warm up.
One morning, about two weeks before the
end of term, it was so hot that Mr Majeika
opened the windows in Class Three. For some
reason Hamish Bigmore seemed very pleased
at this, though no one could make out why.

Mr Majeika was in charge of school dinner that day, and he walked up and down between the tables, making sure that everyone was eating tidily and not making a mess. Hamish Bigmore was being unusually nice to him. 'Oh, Mr Magic,' he kept saying, 'isn't it a lovely day? I do hope you're feeling well today?'

'Yes, thank you, Hamish,' said Mr Majeika, obviously pleased that Hamish was being polite.

'Is there anything I can get you?' Hamish asked, smiling sweetly. 'I'm sure the dinner-ladies would give me a cup of tea for you if I asked them nicely. Shall I go to the kitchen and see?'

Mr Majeika smiled back at Hamish. 'That's very kind of you,' he said. 'Yes, I would love a cup of tea if they can make me one without too much trouble.' And off went Hamish.

A few minutes later he came back, carrying the tea. 'Here you are, Mr Magic,' he said, still smiling sweetly. 'I do hope you like it.'

'Thank you, Hamish,' said Mr Majeika, putting it down on the table to let it cool before drinking it.

At this moment Mr Potter bustled up. 'Ah, Mr Majeika, I wonder if we could do a bit of a change-round this afternoon? I haven't seen much of Class Three this term, so I'd like to take them after lunch, and you can take Class

Four, whom I'd normally be teaching. Will that be all right?'

'Certainly,' said Mr Majeika.

'That's fine,' said Mr Potter, and he was just going when he saw the cup of tea. 'Ah,' he said, rather puzzled. 'I see the dinner-ladies have left my tea out here today. I always have a cup of tea after lunch, you know. Wakes me up!' And with that, he downed the tea at one gulp, muttered 'Far too much sugar,' and hurried back to his office.

Hamish Bigmore had gone rather pale. 'What's the matter?' Pete asked him.

Hamish said nothing. But a moment later, after Mr Majeika had gone off to teach Class Four, he whispered to Pete: 'We're for it now! Really for it!'

'What do you mean?' asked Pete.

'That cup of tea!' said Hamish. 'It was meant for Mr Magic.'

'I know that,' said Pete. 'But I don't think he really minded Mr Potter drinking it.'

'It's not that, you ass,' said Hamish. *There was flying potion in it.*

'*What?*' shouted Pete.

'Ssh!' said Hamish. 'I meant it for Mr Majeika. I thought I'd get my own back for being turned into a frog, so I hid the flying potion and meant to make him drink it all one day when the window was open, and I hoped he'd fly away out of the window and never come back. And now Mr Potter's drunk it instead!'

'Was there a lot in the cup?' asked Pete.

'The whole bottle,' said Hamish gloomily. 'I can't imagine what's going to happen.'

Pete thought for a few moments. Then he said: 'If odd things start to happen to Mr Potter, we'll *all* get into trouble, you can be sure of that. And if he finds out that Mr Magic's flying potion is at the back of it, you can be sure Mr Magic will lose his job, and Class Three will be given an ordinary teacher instead. Now, that may be what *you* want, Hamish Bigmore, but the rest of us certainly don't. So I'm going to warn everyone *not to pay any attention if Mr Potter starts to fly*. It's the only hope ...'

When Mr Potter arrived to teach Class Three fifteen minutes later, everyone had been warned. They sat silently at their desks, knowing that something very odd was probably going to happen, but determined not to laugh or give any other sign that something extraordinary was going on.

In fact, for a very long time nothing happened at all. Mr Potter began to give them an ordinary, boring lesson, and the afternoon dragged by as slowly as usual.

'It takes half an hour to work,' Jody whispered to Thomas. 'The flying potion, I mean.'

'The half hour was up a long time ago,' whispered Thomas. 'I can't think why nothing's happening.'

'*I* know,' whispered Pete. 'It's because he's not *thinking* about flying. You've got to think about it in order to leave the ground.'

'Well, let's hope he *doesn't* think about it,' whispered Pandora.

Mr Potter glanced up irritably. 'Stop that

whispering at the back!' he said. 'Has any of you been listening to me? What have I been talking about, Jody?'

There was an awkward silence as Jody tried to remember what Mr Potter had been saying. 'It was something about how the wind works, wasn't it?' she asked hopefully.

'Certainly not!' spluttered Mr Potter. 'I have been giving you a lesson on the force of gravity. Do you know what gravity is?'

Jody shook her head.

'Oh, really!' said Mr Potter. 'You haven't been listening at all. Gravity is the thing which keeps us all on the ground, and stops us floating up *into the air* ...'

His voice became a squeak of surprise on these last three words, for as he spoke them, he himself left the floor and began to rise slowly towards the ceiling.

There were a few snufflings among Class
Three as they stuffed handkerchieves into
their mouths to stop themselves laughing.
But otherwise, silence.

Mr Potter had stopped rising, and was
suspended in mid-air, about four feet from
the floor. 'Er,' he said, 'something peculiar
seems to have . . .' He looked at Class Three,
and Class Three looked back at him. No one
laughed or said anything. Slowly, Mr Potter
came down to the ground.

'He must have stopped thinking about floating,' whispered Jody. 'Let's make him talk about something else. That should keep his mind off it.'

'Mr Potter,' said Thomas loudly, 'we don't really want to hear any more about the force of gravity. Why not tell us about winds instead?'

'Certainly not!' said Mr Potter crossly. 'Kindly attend to the lesson. As I was saying, gravity stops us from floating in the air. Now you may ask how it is that birds manage to fly? Let me tell you. When birds wave their wings —' He started to wave his arms to show them what he meant; and, as he did so, he rose once more in the air. At first he didn't seem to notice, and simply went on talking.

'By moving their wings,' he said, 'birds create a current of air which permits them to fly wherever they want. They can fly to the left' (and so saying, Mr Potter flew across the classroom) 'or to the right' (he flew back to his desk) 'or round and round in circles.'

As he said these last words, Mr Potter slowly circled the room, and then returned to his desk. He looked puzzled. 'Er,' he said, 'I don't know how to put this, boys and girls, but during the last few minutes, while I was talking to you, I had the strange sensation that ... well, that *I* was flying like a bird. Did you notice anything odd, boys and girls?'

'Oh no,' said Thomas.

'We didn't see a thing,' said Pete.

'You must have imagined it,' said Jody.

'Only,' said Thomas, 'we wish you'd stop thinking about – I mean talking about – flying, and tell us about something else.'

'Listen, boy,' said Mr Potter crossly, 'I am going to finish my lesson on the force of gravity, and I want no more interruptions from you! Now you must understand that, if it were not for the force of gravity, we couldn't simply walk about on two legs. Why, we'd often find ourselves standing on our heads!' And of course, as he said these words, Mr Potter's feet rose a little from the ground and he slowly turned right over in the air, coming to rest standing on his head.

There was silence. 'Are you *sure* nothing peculiar is happening to me, boys and girls?' came Mr Potter's voice from the floor.

'Oh, nothing at all,' said Pandora Green. 'You're just standing by your desk as usual.'

'Oh,' said Mr Potter. 'Oh well ... I really ought to go and see a doctor about these funny things I keep imagining ... Still, I must finish the lesson.' He cleared his throat. 'Not only would we often find ourselves standing on our heads,' he continued, 'but without gravity we could simply float out through any open window, sail up into the sky, and never come back.'

And of course, exactly as these words left Mr Potter's lips, he left the floor and began to float, still upside-down, towards the open window.

'Quick!' shouted Pete. 'Someone shut the window, or he'll never be seen again.'

Everyone made a rush for the window. But just at that moment the bell rang for the end of afternoon school; and as it did so, Mr Potter came back to earth with a bump and sat up, rubbing his head.

'Good gracious!' he said. 'What a lot of funny things I have been imagining. Boys and girls, back to your places! I never said you could go yet.'

'The half-hour's up!' whispered Jody. 'The flying potion has worn off. Thank goodness for that!'

The door opened, and in came Mr Majeika. He was holding something in his hand. 'I hope they behaved themselves?' he asked Mr Potter, who nodded rather weakly. 'That's good,' said Mr Majeika. 'I found *this* in the kitchen.' He showed Class Three what was in his hand; it was the empty bottle which had contained the flying potion. 'I just wondered if anyone had been ...?' he said, looking at them meaningfully.

Class Three shook their heads.

'Nothing's happened at all, Mr Magic,' said Hamish Bigmore firmly. 'It was just an ordinary lesson. But I think Mr Potter would like a cup of tea to calm his nerves. And no sugar in it this time.'

7. Dental Problems

'Mr Potter wants everyone to clean their teeth very thoroughly tomorrow,' said Mr Majeika to Class Three, one afternoon about a week before the end of term. 'There's a dentist coming to teach you about careful brushing, and how to fight tooth decay, and Mr Potter says he doesn't want everyone's mouths looking and smelling like the insides of old dustbins.'

'Please, Mr Magic, my teeth are *always* clean,' said a voice. It was Melanie.

'Yes, Melanie, I'm sure they are,' said Mr Majeika. 'But not everyone is as careful as you.'

'Melanie's teeth are *clean* all right,' said Hamish Bigmore. 'But look how ugly they are! They stick out all over the place.'

Unfortunately this was quite true. Melanie did have sticking-out teeth. But of course being told this made her cry even louder than usual. 'Boo-hoo! I hate you, Hamish Bigmore, you're *horrid*!' she wailed.

'Don't you call *me* horrid,' answered Hamish. 'Just think how horrid *you* look, with those teeth. In fact you look just like Count Dracula! Melanie's got teeth like a vampire! Ya, horrid old vampire!'

'Be quiet, Hamish Bigmore,' said Mr Majeika. But Hamish, as usual, wouldn't pay any attention. 'Vampire! Vampire!' he shouted. 'Melanie looks like a vampire!'

Mr Majeika suddenly lost his temper. 'I'll show you who's a vampire!' he cried, and pointed a finger at Hamish.

Hamish Bigmore opened his mouth to say something rude – and then stopped, because everyone was suddenly laughing at him. 'Vampire! Vampire!' they were shouting.

'What's got into you, you sillies?' he asked them. But they would only answer: 'Vampire! Vampire!'

'Here,' said Pandora Green, 'take a look at this.' She kept a pocket-mirror in her desk for putting on lipstick, when Mr Majeika wasn't looking. Now she held it up to Hamish Bigmore.

He stared in the mirror, then turned on Mr Majeika. 'Look what you've done, Mr Magic!' he shouted.

It was perfectly true. Hamish Bigmore had suddenly grown vampire's teeth.

They were very long and pointed, and stuck right out of his mouth. Two were especially long and sharp. It was as nasty a sight as anything in the horror films on television.

'Oh dear, oh dear,' Mr Majeika was saying. 'I seem to have done it again. These old spells just come back into my head when I least expect them, and then I say them to myself without thinking, and then hey presto! the damage is done.'

'But surely you know how to take *this* spell off him?' asked Jody. 'It can't be as difficult as the frog.'

Mr Majeika shook his head. 'It's quite an

easy one,' he said. 'In fact you don't need a spell to get rid of the vampire teeth, I remember that. Hamish himself has to *do* something to have his teeth become normal again. But I can't for the life of me think what it is.'

Hamish Bigmore himself had been sitting silently through this. Now he snarled between his vampire teeth: 'Well, if you can't take these teeth away, I'm going to *use* them. I'll be a real vampire and bite you all! And you know what happens when you're bitten by a vampire? You become a vampire yourself! Ha! ha!'

'Don't be silly,' said Mr Majeika. 'You're not a real vampire. You just happen to have grown a set of vampire's teeth. But I can tell you that if you start behaving in a foolish fashion, Hamish Bigmore, you can be sure of one thing – those teeth will never go away.

Just you put a scarf around your face to hide them, and go home quietly, and tell everyone there that you've got toothache, and go straight to bed, and with luck in the morning they'll have gone.'

For once, Hamish Bigmore did as he was told.

But the next morning the vampire teeth were still there. Thomas and Pete could see them the moment Hamish Bigmore came into Class Three and unwrapped the scarf from around his face. 'Whatever did your mum and dad say?' asked Pete.

'They're away,' said Hamish. 'There's an old aunt of mine looking after me, and she's too short-sighted to notice. Mr Magic should go to prison for doing this to me!'

'It was all your own fault,' said Thomas. 'But what is the dentist going to say?'

This was exactly the thought that crossed Mr Majeika's mind when he arrived in the classroom and saw that Hamish's teeth hadn't changed back in the night. 'Oh dear,' he said, 'this is going to be very awkward.'

When the dentist came, it proved to be a lady. Hamish Bigmore had been put in a far corner of the room, in the hope that she would not look at him, but she went carefully round everyone in the class, making them all open their mouths.

'Now,' she said brightly, peering into Thomas's, 'have you been brushing away regularly with Betty Brush and Tommy Toothpaste? You must remember to fight Dan Decay, and Percy Plaque, or horrid old Terry Toothache will come along and make your life a misery.'

'She's treating us as if we were toddlers in the nursery class,' grumbled Jody. But there was nothing anyone could do to stop the lady dentist chattering away in this daft fashion. Finally she got to Hamish Bigmore, who, on Mr Majeika's instructions, had the scarf wrapped tightly around his mouth.

'Who have we here?' she said brightly. Hamish got to his feet and started to make for the door.

'He's not feeling very well,' said Mr Majeika. 'I think he needs to go to the lavatory.'

'Well, he can just wait a minute,' said the lady dentist firmly. 'Let's unwrap that scarf, my little friend, and see what we find beneath. Are Dan Decay and Percy Plaque lurking there, or have you been a good boy and used Betty Brush and Tommy Toothpaste?'

Hamish Bigmore had had enough of this. He pulled the scarf from his face and bared his horrid long pointed teeth at the lady dentist.

'No,' he cried. 'I haven't been a good boy!
I'm Victor the Vampire and I'm going to
drink your blood!'

The lady dentist gave a shrill scream, and
rushed from the classroom.

*

'Now really,' said Mr Majeika to Hamish
Bigmore when order had been restored, 'that
was *not* necessary. You might have given her
a heart attack.' As it was, the lady dentist had
driven away very fast in her little car, saying
she never wanted to look at schoolchildren's
teeth again.

'I'm sorry you've still got those teeth,'
continued Mr Majeika to Hamish, 'but really,
behaving so naughtily won't help. I'm still
trying to find out what it is you must do to
get rid of them — I've been looking through
all my old spell-books — and in the meantime
I advise you to be as good as possible ...'

Suddenly he stopped.

'What's the matter?' asked Jody.

'I've just remembered!' cried Mr Majeika in delight. 'I've remembered what Hamish has to do to get rid of those teeth! *He has to be good!*'

8. Hamish the Good

At first no one could believe it was as simple as that. But in the end Mr Majeika convinced them all. 'I've remembered what I was taught as an apprentice wizard,' he said. 'If anyone gets a horrid affliction or disease as a result of behaving nastily to someone,' he said, 'they have to be *good* for a certain period of time, and it will go away. So Hamish will have to be good until — well, I should think until the end of term should just about do it. What do you think about that, Hamish?'

Hamish Bigmore looked at Mr Majeika gloomily. 'Isn't there an easier way?' he said.

Mr Majeika shook his head. 'I'm afraid not,' he said. 'For the next week or so, Hamish, you will have to behave like an entirely different person. You must become utterly and completely *good*.'

Hamish sat in silence, stunned by this news.

'He'll never manage it,' said Pete to Thomas. 'Not a hope.'

*

But the surprising thing was that, by next day, Hamish obviously *was* managing it.

Up to now, he had always arrived late at school in the morning, with some silly excuse he'd dreamt up. But today Class Three found him already sitting at his desk when they arrived. And when Mr Majeika came into the classroom, he saw that there was a bunch of wild flowers in a jam jar on his table. 'Oh,' he said. 'Did one of the girls put this here?'

There was a general shaking of heads, and Hamish spoke up: 'No, sir' (he had never called Mr Majeika or any of the other teachers 'sir' before), 'it was me, sir. I picked them from the hedgerow on my way to school. Don't you think they're pretty, sir?'

Mr Majeika looked at Hamish Bigmore suspiciously. 'Don't overdo it, Hamish,' he said warningly. 'Just being *normally* good, like everyone else, will be quite enough.' But Hamish said nothing.

They began lessons. Normally Hamish Bigmore interrupted Mr Majeika at least once every five minutes, with some silly question or rude comment. But today he was completely silent. Mr Majeika obviously couldn't believe it, for he kept casting uneasy glances in Hamish's direction to make sure he wasn't up to something nasty. But not at all. Hamish was very hard at work, and at the end of the lesson he handed a neatly written workbook to Mr Majeika. Class Three had been asked to write something describing a scene in the country, and Hamish's piece was all about sweet little buttercups, and little woolly lambs jumping about in the meadows. 'Are you trying to pull my leg, Hamish Bigmore?' said Mr Majeika. But once again Hamish made no reply.

It was the same at dinner time. Mr Majeika had explained to Mr Potter and the rest of the school that something peculiar had happened to Hamish's teeth, but they would soon be all right again providing nobody took any notice; so Hamish was allowed to have school dinner with everyone else. Usually he fooled around like mad at dinner time, and made a dreadful nuisance of himself to the dinner-ladies. But today everything was different. He not only ate his own dinner as quietly as a mouse, but after it was finished he began to collect up all the other children's dirty plates, knives, forks, and spoons, saying to the dinner-ladies: 'Oh, *do* let me help! Please, is there anything I can do?'

After a bit, one of the dinner-ladies went to Mr Majeika to complain. 'That boy from your class,' she said, 'is giving us all the creeps.'

'Do you mean his teeth?' asked Mr Majeika.

'No, he can't help those, poor dear,' said the dinner-lady. 'I mean his *interference*. He doesn't mean to be a nuisance, the poor creature, but he keeps fussing round us, trying to *help* all the time, and we can't get the washing-up done. What's wrong with him? The other kids never behave like that.'

Mr Majeika sighed. 'I'm afraid he's

suffering from an attack of being good,' he
said.

Nor was this the end of Hamish Bigmore's
'helping'. At the end of afternoon school he
hurried round to the nursery class, and was
soon to be seen 'helping' the little children
on with their coats, and holding the door
open for the mothers who had come to
collect them. Unfortunately nobody in the
nursery had been told about Hamish
Bigmore's vampire teeth, and the air was
soon filled with the screams of terrified
mothers. 'It's Dracula himself, risen from the
grave!' cried one of the more highly-strung
ladies. Mr Majeika, summoned to the
disturbance, told Hamish Bigmore to stop
'helping', and to go home at once, but the
damage was done, and it was several days
before some of the mothers would venture
out of doors again with their toddlers.

Every day for a week, Hamish Bigmore thought of some new way of 'helping' someone at St Barty's, and by the end of the week everyone in the school was a nervous wreck. Everyone, that is, except Mr Potter. Somehow Hamish's good deeds had failed to cause any trouble to the head teacher.

On the last morning of term, Hamish Bigmore arrived at school with his teeth looking perfectly normal again. And there was a gleam in his eye. 'Well, I think I've managed it,' he said to Pete and Thomas.

'Your teeth?' they said. 'Yes, you have. They look quite ordinary again. Mr Majeika was right, then – it worked.'

'No, not *that*, idiots,' said Hamish Bigmore scornfully. And his 'goodness' seemed to have vanished now that his teeth were back to normal. 'Just you wait and see what I mean.'

The day ended with the whole school gathered in the assembly hall to listen to Mr Potter. 'I want you all to enjoy your holidays,' he said. 'But before you go, there's one last thing. Those of you who have been at St Barty's for some time will know that on the last day of the Easter term I always give a prize, the Headmaster's Medal for Good Conduct. And as you may also know, beside the medal there's also ten pounds in cash for the boy or girl who wins it. Each year I look for one boy or girl whose behaviour has been really good, and who has tried to be a real help to everyone at the school. And this term, I have no hesitation in awarding the prize to – Hamish Bigmore.'

There was a gasp of surprise and, especially from Class Three, a howl of rage.

'So *that's* what he was up to,' gasped Pete. 'He didn't care about the teeth at all –

he just wanted the money! Well of all
the –'

'Jolly well done, Hamish Bigmore,' said
Mr Potter, hanging the medal round
Hamish's neck and giving him an envelope
containing the money.

'Thank you, *sir*,' said Hamish Bigmore.
And he stuck out his tongue at Class Three.

After it was all over, everyone crowded
round Mr Majeika. 'Wasn't that wicked of
Hamish Bigmore?' Jody asked him. 'Did you
know what he was up to?'

Mr Majeika shook his head. 'I'd never heard of this Good Conduct Medal,' he said, 'or I might have guessed. Why, for two pins I'd turn that medal into a toad!'

'Oh, go on, Mr Magic, please do!' they all said. But he shook his head.

'No, my friends. No more magic, at least not this term.'

'Will you be here *next* term, Mr Magic?' Jody asked excitedly.

Mr Majeika nodded.

'Hooray!' they all said. And then Thomas added as an afterthought:

'Well, don't let Hamish Bigmore ever be *good* again. It's more than we can bear!'